Violet's Music

by

ANGELA JOHNSON

illustrated by

LAURA HULISKA-BEITH

Dial Books for Young Readers **New York**

For Sam, Maggie, and Annie — A. J.

For Jeff — L.H.B.

Published by Dial Books for Young Readers
A division of Penguin Young Readers Group
345 Hudson Street
New York, New York 10014

Text copyright © 2004 by Angela Johnson
Illustrations copyright © 2004 by Laura Huliska-Beith
All rights reserved
Designed by Lily Malcom
Text set in Rockwell Bold
Manufactured in China on acid-free paper

11

Library of Congress Cataloging-in-Publication Data
Johnson, Angela, date.
Violet's music / Angela Johnson ; illustrated by Laura Huliska-Beith.
p. cm.
Summary: From the days she banged her rattle in the crib,
Violet has been looking for friends to share her love of music.
ISBN 978-0-8037-2740-3
[1. Musicians—Fiction. 2. Bands—Fiction.]
I. Huliska-Beith, Laura, ill. II. Title.
PZ7J629Vi 2004
[E]—dc21
2003002037

The illustrations for this book were done in acrylic,
collaged paper, and fabric on Strathmore paper.

When Violet was a baby,
just a few hours old,

she banged her rattle
against the crib,
hoping others in the
nursery would join in.

Boom
Shake
Beat
Shake

**All day long,
Violet played that rattle.**

Could she find other babies to play along?
No, she couldn't.
But she'd keep looking.
Violet played her music all alone.

On Violet's second birthday
Aunt Bertha brought gifts
and a box full of paper, crayons,
glitter, and glue
to make horns that would wail . . .

Violet tooted from morning till that night.

WHAH

WOO

WOO

All day long.

She tried to get everyone to toot with her all day.

WHAH
  WOO
   WOO

Oh yeah.
Violet blew that horn.

Could she get her family
to play with her?
No, she couldn't.
But she'd keep on looking.

Violet blew her horn all alone.

Violet wondered in kindergarten
if there were other kids like her,
who dreamed music,
thought music,
all day long.

But she found that
some liked to paint,
some liked to paste,
others liked to play in the sandbox,
and still others just liked to stand around eating paste.

No one wanted to play music all day long.

One day at the beach
Violet played with a badminton racket,
a pretend guitar,
hoping someone would join in.

Plink
   Plink
Pluck
   Pluck

Violet played guitar.

Could she find a fellow guitarist buried in the sand?
No, she couldn't.
But she'd keep looking.
Violet played her guitar all alone.

With Violet, you see, it was music all the time.

Breakfast time . . .

Dinner time . . .

Bath time . . .

And all times in between.

Whenever she walked down the street
or hid behind the market's vegetable bins,
or sat on the fire escape,
Violet was always looking for kids like her.

Could she find them at the zoo?
Nope.

At the museum?
Too quiet.

And forget about the dentist.

But she'd keep looking.
Violet and her music, always looking.

Until . . .
one day a few summers later,
Violet was playing her guitar
(a real one now)
in the park.

Twang
    Twang
Yeah
    Yeah
Twang Twang
    Yeah!

When, over by the fountain,
someone started beating a drum . . .

Then, behind the jungle gym,
a saxophone blew real smooth . . .

And over beside the flower garden,
someone started to sing . . .

Now Angel, Randy, and Juan
are in Violet's band.
And if you ask any of them
whether they thought they'd find each other,
they'll say,
"Oh yeah, we did, we knew we would.

'Cause when we were in the nursery,

then were two,

and later in kindergarten
and at the beach,
we kept on looking
for kids playing music too!"

Shake TWANG PLINK Pluck WHAH Woo YEAH!